The
Red Castle
&
The Blue

The
Red Castle
&
The Blue

WENDY MARECH

WITH ILLUSTRATIONS BY
ALAYNA E. PAQUETTE

MARLOE PRESS

The Red Castle and the Blue

Copyright © 2018 Marloe Press

ISBN 978-0-9823495-5-7

Printed and bound in the U.S.A.

Designed and composed by
Gretchen Achilles/Wavetrap Design

Cover design by Jenny Carrow

www.marloepress.com

The
Red Castle
&
The Blue

CHAPTER ONE

The Plan

Once upon a time—for that is how most stories about princes and princesses and castles and kidnappings and brave knights and masked men and bold escapes begin…

But forgive me; I am getting ahead of myself.

As I was saying, once upon a time, there was a blue castle. In the time when this story takes place, castles were often but one part of what we would today call

a walled city—which is, not surprisingly, a city surrounded by walls. In times of great danger, the gates in those walls would be locked up tight, but in peaceful times, as was then the case, they stood open and people could come and go as they pleased.

Of course, most castles at the time were ruled by kings, and this castle was no different. In the blue castle, there lived the blue king, who was a good sort of king, and his daughter, the blue Princess Azula. Many princesses are said to be quite beautiful—most of them, in fact—and so it was with Azula. She was, many claimed, as beautiful as the moon—which, as you know from looking out your window at night, is pale and lovely. And maybe she was, and maybe she wasn't; you be the judge.

Because everyone said these things, word of Azula's beauty leaked out of the castle and traveled far and wide. Sometimes it traveled with a knight on the back

AZULA

of a horse; sometimes in a wagon with a family of four; sometimes even on foot with a traveling salesman; but however it managed to get around, get around it did.

Now in this story, as in many others, not everyone is good and kind and gentle—for such is the way of the world—and a lot of *these* people lived in another castle, several kingdoms and one small mountain range away. This castle was known as the red castle, a name you yourself might have given it had you seen it first, for its walls, in addition to being high and wide, were also red. See—here is a picture.

In this castle, among the people who grew the flowers and pruned the trees and cooked the food and fixed the plumbing and wired the lights—because even in those days, a castle had to have lights—there lived the

THE RED
KING

THE RED
QUEEN

red king and his wife, the red queen, and their three sons who were named, in order, Rouget, Rojar, and Harold. These three were, naturally, princes and two of them—Rouget and Rojar—were of the not-very-nice variety.

As children, they had also not been very nice. They had called the other children names, and hit them when the grown-ups weren't looking, and taken their toys

ROUGET   ROJAR   HAROLD

and sweets and generally misbehaved in ways that I am
sure *you* never do. And of course they had grown up to
be just the kind of people you'd expect those children
to become. So if you'd like a bit of advice—and certainly there are plenty of people who would not—try
not to be that kind of child, for you just may turn into
that kind of grown-up whom no one likes very much,
only they are too polite to say.

13

But to return to our story, word of the moon-beautiful Azula spread far and wide. And after he had heard of her great beauty for the sixth or the twelfth or the twenty-fifth time, Prince Rouget decided that what he wanted more than anything else in the whole wide world was the Princess Azula. And as he had gotten nearly everything else he had ever wanted, why not a princess? After all, doesn't every prince deserve one? To be fair, you'd have to ask the princesses. But we shall leave that for another day.

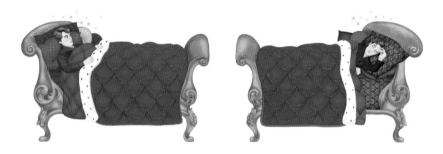

"Rojar," whispered Prince Rouget one night when they had gone to bed. The two shared a room, which made talking after bedtime easy.

Rojar pretended to be asleep. He let out a small sigh that was supposed to be his sleeping sound.

But Rouget knew better. "Rojar," he said again, a little louder. "Rojar."

Rojar let out another sigh, which was his not-sleeping sound.

"I must have her," Rouget continued.

"Who?" Rojar asked, thoroughly awake. "Who must you have?"

"The beautiful Azula."

Rojar sat up on his elbow. "Why?"

"Because I want to marry her."

"But how do you intend to get her?"

Rouget thought a moment. "I shall send someone to fetch her."

"I don't think it works that way. Besides, her father may have someone else in mind for her."

"Then what can I do?" Rouget sighed dramatically. "Because I must have her. I must."

Rojar considered. "I would think you need a plan," he said. Of the two, he was the more cunning.

"I know that," said Rouget in that annoyed tone older brothers always seem to use with younger ones. "But I can't think of one."

"Then I will," said Rojar. And that is just what he did.

Azula, of course, knew nothing of this plan, nor of the princes themselves. She was busy leading the kind of life that princesses are supposed to lead: buying fine clothes, eating fine foods, going on fine expeditions and, in general, having a fine time without doing any of the hard work most people must do to earn it. But even having a fine time can become dull when it is all you have to do.

So it should come as no surprise that one bright market day, when two young merchants selling toys out of a gay red gypsy wagon set up shop, Azula was most interested to see their wares.

She did not often go to the market, for there were other people in the castle whose job it was to do such things, just as there were other people whose job it was to do most everything. But as they were all busy doing those things, Azula was able to slip away without anybody asking where she was going or what she was doing—questions which, in general, may be rather annoying, but if you are a princess or a child are probably, when all is said and done, a good thing.

Now the merchants, as you may have guessed, were none other than the princes Rouget and Rojar. They had been waiting for the princess since the sun came up, and they were bored.

"Where is she?" asked Rouget impatiently. "Hasn't she heard we have a wagon full of toys?"

"Perhaps she hasn't," said Rojar, who had been thinking the same thing.

"Then someone ought to tell her."

But there was no need. For at that very moment, Azula herself came strolling down the cobbled street.

"Look." Rojar nudged Rouget. "It is the princess."

You may ask how he knew this, for neither prince had ever seen Azula before and the red castle, although it had a cappuccino machine, was not equipped with televisions or computers or smartphones or any of those other devices that we today use to figure out who is who. But it was easy. For Azula, the blue princess, had on the most beautiful blue dress, and she looked very different from the other people who wore, as you and I might, jeans and dirty sneakers. People's clothing, at the time, said a great deal about who they were.

The two princes watched her.

"She is not," said Rouget critically, "as beautiful as the moon."

"But she is still quite pretty," said Rojar encouragingly. It would be a shame to scrap his plan just now, before he'd even had a chance to see how well it worked.

Rouget studied the princess. "To be honest," he continued, "she is something of a disappointment."

"She's exactly what a princess ought to be," Rojar said soothingly. "Look at her jewels. Look at her dress. She is a princess through and through."

"And yet I find her lacking."

"Do you wish to find another princess?" asked Rojar, who hoped his brother didn't.

"No." Rouget sighed.

"Then I think you must be satisfied with this one."

"Is there no alternative?"

"None whatsoever," Rojar answered firmly.

"Oh, all right," Rouget relented. "I will have her. Though she isn't nearly what I'd hoped for."

"Hush," his brother whispered. "Here she comes."

Azula swept into the princes' stall.

"We are most honored." Rouget bowed and bit his tongue. For what he wished to say was that it was about time and how long were they going to have to wait. "It isn't often we are visited by princesses."

"It isn't often there is anything to visit," said Azula, picking up a monkey with brass cymbals.

"We have many fine toys," said Rouget, for he had raided all his castle's toy chests, and those of the kingdom's other children, too.

"Indeed you do." Azula touched a globe, which gently spun about its axis. "Look how big the world is," she said. She herself had never been outside the castle's walls.

"We also have a music box," Rouget said, thrusting it into her hands. It was his globe, and he didn't like her touching it.

Azula took the music box and turned the key. The lid sprang open to reveal a dancing bear spinning in circles.

"Do you like it?" asked Rouget.

"I like it very much," Azula said.

"Before you set your heart on it," said Rojar slyly, "let us show you something else. We only rarely show it."

"What is it?" the princess asked with interest.

"It's our circus set."

"Our what?" said Rouget.

"Our circus set," said Rojar, elbowing his brother. For of course there was no circus set. It was a trick.

"Oh, yes," said Rouget. "The one with the acrobats and the trapezes and the elephants and clowns and dogs and horses."

"And two lions," Rojar added, for he wanted to be sure the toy sounded tremendous. "Would you like to see it?"

"May I?" asked Azula.

"Certainly. But you will have to step inside the wagon."

Now you might think it very silly of the princess to do so, and I am certain, given all your parents tell you about not trusting strangers, you would never do the same yourself. But then Azula was a princess and a princess, in addition to leading a very different kind of life than you and I, never seems to get half the useful lessons that the rest of us must swallow every day with breakfast. So, of course, she stepped into the wagon.

"It is very dark in here," she said.

"Give it a moment. Let your eyes adjust."

Azula blinked.

"Now I will turn the lamp on very slowly," said Rojar. "And I will sweeten the air with a small drop of perfume."

But it wasn't perfume he sprayed. It was a sleeping potion.

"What a funny smell," Azula said. She yawned and sat down and was suddenly asleep.

The afternoon passed very slowly for Rouget and Rojar. At any moment, they expected a blue knight to gallop through the market, find out what they'd done, and haul them to the dungeon. Rojar's heart thumped loudly every time a customer came to the stall, and Rouget hummed a wedding march under his breath to calm himself. And naturally, from time to time, they both peeked in the back at their new treasure, hoping no one had yet noticed she had disappeared.

But they needn't have worried. For the princess had told no one of her plans, which meant no one knew she had gone missing.

Finally, the castle's clock struck four, and all the merchants packed their wares.

The princes didn't want to be the first to leave. But they were second. As soon as the castle's gate was out of sight, they spurred their horses to a gallop and went hurtling across the kingdom, clumps of dirt and grass flying beneath them and the little wagon rattling merrily behind.

"We've done it!" cried Rouget, his eyes shining with excitement.

And indeed they had.

CHAPTER TWO

The Rescue

Now if this were an ordinary story, sometime during the journey to the red castle a handsome prince, or fearless knight, or even just a passerby would spot the wagon, discover its unwilling passenger, and rescue our moon-beautiful princess. But this is not that kind of story—or, at any rate, not quite that kind of story. Without any interference, Rouget and Rojar carted their princess through the several kingdoms and across the one small mountain range, snuck her through their castle's gate, and locked her in a tower.

Of course, planning to kidnap a princess and actually having a princess on your hands are two entirely different matters, and suddenly the princes found they had more of a project than they'd bargained for. For now they had to feed their prisoner, and find her clothes, and get her bubble bath and magazines and fluffy towels as befits a princess.

Also, there was the small matter of the king and queen, who weren't yet aware of their sons' expedition and who might not be as thrilled with it as one might hope.

All in all, Rouget thought, standing just outside Azula's door, this kidnapping business was much more work than he'd anticipated. Here he was, expecting happy ever after, and instead he found himself running around the castle, fetching nail polish and scented soap and spray-on glitter for his future bride. It was absurd.

Clearing his throat, he knocked once, unlocked the door, and entered.

"Go away," Azula said. She turned to face the window.

"Is that any way to treat your prince?"

"My what?"

"Your prince."

Azula glared at him. "You're not my prince," she said.

"I am," said Rouget. "I am Prince Rouget. And I intend to marry you."

"I'll never marry you," Azula said. "Never." She spun around and marched into the bathroom, slamming the door behind her for good measure.

Rouget left the tower in a temper. This princess was not behaving as she ought to be. This princess was supposed to be elated—which means happy and excited—that a prince like him would want to take her as his bride.

"She'll come around," said Rojar, who was waiting downstairs.

"But," said Rouget, who was finding the whole matter of his marriage doubtful, "how can you be sure?"

"She is our prisoner," said Rojar. "She has to do what we tell her to."

"Can we tell her to marry me?"

"Of course we can. That's why we kidnapped her," said Rojar reasonably. "Isn't it?"

"It is," said Rouget. And he smiled. He would marry the blue princess yet, and there was nothing she could do about it.

Upstairs in the tower, Azula sat beneath the window, watching a cloud float across the sky and humming a sad song. She didn't like being a prisoner. She didn't like the rose-red nail polish, the scratchy sheets, the dated fashion magazines. She missed her castle, and her father, and her clothes. And she was lonely, too.

A few sad tears slipped down her cheek. Had anyone gone looking for her? Surely, someone must have noticed she was gone. She watched a crow spin lazy circles in the sky and felt quite sorry for herself.

But after several minutes, this grew tiresome. There must be something else to do. She wiped the tears away. Perhaps she'd have another look around.

There hadn't been that much to see the first time she had looked: an ancient dresser, dust under the bed, and one small closet in which three not-very-pretty dresses hung. She peered again into the closet. This time, on the shelf beside the extra comforter, she spied a long black case, inside of which she found, to her surprise, a sword. It was a toy sword, to be sure, but it was nonetheless a sword.

She'd never held a sword before—not even a toy. She picked it up and boldly swished it through the air. One-two; one-two. It felt remarkably good.

Maybe she could use it.

At this juncture in the story, you might wonder what was happening inside the blue castle. I would, if I were you. So let us see.

Azula's absence had at last been noticed. Though at first the staff simply assumed her to be elsewhere—in the gardens, for example, or under the grape arbor or maybe deep inside one of her many walk-in closets— gradually it dawned on everyone that something just a bit more serious might be afoot. For when the princess failed to show up for her teatime, then for dinner, it became quite clear she wasn't just enjoying some alone time. She was missing.

Then—and only then—did the alarm go up.

The king did not cry out 'My kingdom for my princess,' as perhaps *your* parents might were they to find *you* missing. Then again, the king had a whole kingdom to consider—and, more to the point, he had a lot of other kingdoms to consider. To make sure these other kingdoms didn't think the worst of him, he had to pretend that all was well—although, of course, it wasn't. This is what we grown-ups would call international relations—or how kings and kingdoms treat each other.

On the other hand, the missing person was his daughter. Politics aside, he felt the need to act—and quickly. In no time at all, a top-notch search-and-rescue party was dispatched.

But it was too late. Azula, snug inside in the gypsy wagon, was already far away.

And to her we shall return.

With a sigh, Azula set the sword down and returned to her position at the window. How long would it take until someone discovered her? A week? A month? A year? Would she never go home? Would she have to marry Rouget? Her heart sank and a salty tear slid from the corner of her eye.

But help was near.

For unbeknownst to her, outside the window hung a microphone. It had not been there for long; indeed, it had only just been dropped down from the room above that morning. But there it hung, picking up her sighs and sad songs and transmitting them, with just a bit of static, to the room above.

You might ask to whom this microphone belonged. Or maybe you can guess. But if not, I shall tell you. Rouget and Rojar, you may remember, had a brother. And this brother—Harold—was as unlike them as apples are from blueberries—which is to say, they're both round, and they're both fruit, but there the similarities end.

Unlike both his brothers, Harold was a decent sort. And because he was considerate, and shared his toys, and waited his turn, and said please and thank you, he did not, to say the least, get on at all with Rouget and Rojar. This caused him no end of trouble, as perhaps you understand from those few times when you have had to be around a person who is bigger than you are, and bossy too.

Through his telescope, Harold had seen his brothers sneaking through the castle, clutching objects tightly to their chests and casting furtive glances here and there. He'd caught them whispering and scurrying through unused doorways. Once, he could have sworn Rouget held something small and glittery; another time, he was convinced he smelled his mother's bath salts, made from real red roses. Something odd was going on. And Harold, naturally, was curious.

Years of having to avoid his brothers had taught him all the ins and outs of the red castle. He knew every room; each staircase; all the corridors; even the deepest, darkest dungeons. So it didn't take long to discover that the object of his brothers' attention was to be found on the sixth floor of the southeast tower;

and it took even less time to discover that this object was, in fact, a princess.

But then it took a whole *lot* of time to figure out what to do with this discovery.

Only after Harold had crept up to the empty room above and carefully lowered the microphone had he been able to understand the princess's predicament— which was, of course, that Rouget planned to marry her despite her very obvious objections. And it was this— even more than the fact that she'd been kidnapped— that was the main sticking point for Harold.

He concluded that someone was going to have to rescue the princess, and there being no one else around, that someone would have to be him.

All night long, he thought and he thought and he thought. And by the next night, when the sun dropped behind the hills beyond the castle and the crescent moon appeared above them, he had come up with a plan.

That night, long after Azula had nibbled at and sent away her dinner—for it is difficult to be satisfied with a peanut-butter-and-jelly sandwich when you are used to eating quiche Lorraine or boeuf Bourguignon or coquilles Saint-Jacques or something equally fancy—Harold, wearing a dark mask, tiptoed down the stairs, unlocked the heavy door, and slowly pushed it open.

But Azula was prepared.

As the door opened, she grabbed the toy sword, leapt across the room, and swung it wildly at the intruder.

"Ouch!" cried Harold. "Watch it with that sword."

Azula stepped back. Someone in a mask was not what she'd expected. "Who are you?" she asked, bewildered.

"I'm your rescuer," said Harold, rubbing his leg. He would have a black-and-blue mark for a week.

"My what?" Azula didn't think she'd heard correctly.

"I'm your rescuer," said Harold once again. "I mean to rescue you."

She eyed him doubtfully.

"Why else would I be here?"

Azula could think of several reasons, none of them good. She had met a few unpleasant characters that week, and she was feeling none too optimistic—which means hopeful—that her would-be rescuer was who he said he was and would do what he promised.

"Look, we haven't got all night," Harold continued.

But Azula wasn't satisfied. "I don't mean to be rude," she said. "But how do I know I can trust you?"

"Me?" said Harold.

"Yes," Azula said. "A man in a mask."

Harold's plan had not included this small hiccup. "I suppose you can't," he said after a moment.

"So then tell me," said Azula, "why should I come with you?"

Harold sighed. It was her rescue after all, and if she didn't want it, there was nothing to be done. "Do you have any other ideas?" he asked her politely.

She had to admit she didn't.

"Then," said Harold, "it appears you're stuck with me. So if you'd like a rescue, I suggest you come along at once. We're on a schedule." Carefully, because his leg still hurt, he stepped aside and held the door.

Azula took a last look at the rose-red wallpaper, the

crimson comforter, the ruby-colored curtains. Then she looked at Harold.

"Well?" he said.

"All right," she said. "I'm coming."

Harold headed up the stairs.

"I don't mean to be difficult," Azula said from several steps below, "but shouldn't we be going *down*?"

"We can't get out that way."

"Why not?"

"Because," said Harold patiently, "we are escaping. Which means we need an escape route."

"Do we really?" asked Azula, feeling a small tingle of excitement.

"Trust me," Harold said. And for the second time that night, she did. It was just as well. For Harold, who knew every corner of the castle, naturally knew all about the secret passage that led to the secret stairway that led to the

secret exit where a sleepy guard paid no attention as they left, his job ordinarily being to keep people out, not in.

In no time at all, the two were clip-clopping through the countryside on an old horse Harold had borrowed, Harold in his mask and Azula in a maid's old uniform that had been stolen from the washroom. At first, I'm sorry to say, she had refused to wear the dress. It was an ugly thing, and itchy too, and not the least bit suited for a princess. But the masked man had insisted and she'd figured, having gotten her this far, he might know something about rescuing a princess. So, although reluctantly, she'd worn it. After all, she'd much rather be free than be well-dressed.

It was a lovely night, though something of an awkward situation. The two barely knew each other and yet here they were, bouncing around together on the back of an old horse. Each, you may be sure, was secretly relieved when the red station finally came into view.

The train was waiting at the platform. Harold's timing had been quite precise. "All aboard," cried the conductor, giving the masked Harold an odd look.

Azula climbed the steps. "However can I thank you?" she asked with a sudden quickening—which means a faster beating—of her heart.

"No need," said Harold, which is what you would expect a prince to say.

"My father will reward you," said Azula. "I'm a princess."

"Yes, of course you are," said Harold, feeling just a little shy.

"Is it that obvious?"

He shrugged—because, of course, it was.

There was an uneasy silence. The train whistled and white smoke puffed from its smokestack.

"Will I ever see you again?" asked Azula, as the wheels began to turn.

"I doubt it," Harold said with a small twinge of something like regret.

But he was wrong.

CHAPTER THREE

The Deficit

As you can imagine, there was a great deal of celebration when the princess alighted in the blue station, looking just a little pale but none the worse for wear. Faster than you can say the blue Princess Azula, she was whisked home to the castle where a scented bath was drawn, fine clothes laid out, and a gourmet meal prepared. She was asked to tell her story over and again, the maids and the ladies-in-waiting and the cook and even the king himself gasping in a

combination of delight and horror when she told them how the masked intruder had burst in, and how she'd stabbed him in the leg; and everyone thanking the stars above while they declared how very lucky she was.

Now you would think she would agree with this assessment. After all, she had escaped two crafty kidnappers and managed to avoid having to marry one of them. And, to be sure, she did agree in part. But here's a funny thing about adventures: sometimes you return from them no different than you were when you set out. But other times, you come home vaguely aware that something has changed and, on reflection, realize that that something happens to be you.

This is where Azula found herself. All her life, she had been waited upon hand and foot, and had had her every whim and fancy satisfied. She'd never laid out her own clothes, or styled her own hair, or even thought much for herself. Then suddenly she found herself out on her own. And here is the most interesting part: she liked it. Don't get me wrong: she didn't like the princes or the sleeping potion or the locked room or the kidnapping. But she had led what we today would call a very sheltered life, which is to say she'd never left her father's kingdom. When she finally did, she found the world outside its borders fascinating.

In the days and weeks that followed, she would

often think back on her journey. She would think about the steam train and the starry sky; the secret passage and the countryside; and most of all, about the masked man who had rescued her. She recalled the taste of peanut butter, which she'd never had before; the scratchy stiffness of the maid's old uniform; and even, if pressed, would admit that she had rather liked the smell of rose bath salts. As you can see, Azula had had one of those adventures which had changed her.

But enough about this for the moment. Our story now continues in the red castle.

Several kingdoms and one mountain range away, Prince Rouget was feeling bitter. Here he'd gone through all this trouble just to get himself a princess, and in the middle of the night she'd up and vanished. Poof. Without a trace—meaning no one had seen her—though, of course, no one *had* seen her.

For Rouget and Rojar hadn't yet gotten around to telling anyone. They'd needed—so Rojar had said—a story—and a quite convincing one at that. And I can tell you, being something of a story-teller myself, that a story is, if not always an amusing thing, certainly a useful one. For stories can explain whatever needs explaining—why you overslept and missed the bus to school;

or how you came to have five candies in your pocket; or even why there is a kidnapped princess locked up in the southeast tower. Without a convincing story—or at least a good one—Rouget and Rojar could not explain Azula's presence. So they hadn't.

And perhaps, now she was gone, they should have left the situation as it was.

But Rouget, who was no longer so certain he wanted to marry Azula—let alone even liked her very much—liked even less that he had been outsmarted. As a prince, he'd always been allowed to win, and this had given him a rather wrong impression of his talents. You and I, of course, know better. *We* know it's nearly impossible to always be a winner, and we understand that if we find ourselves in that position, chances are that something's off.

But Rouget wasn't you or me. Much worse, he was a sore loser. Standing in the now-deserted sixth-floor prison, it was very clear to him that if he were to keep his pride intact—that is, to go on winning—he would have to get the princess back. And soon.

It was just about at this time that the red castle began to have money problems.

A castle, as you may be aware, is an expensive proposition. There are knights and squires and maids and gardeners and cooks and carpenters and dog-walkers and window-washers and painters and plumbers and janitors and jesters and messengers and secretaries and so on and so forth; and each and every one of them has to be paid. Then, of course, there are the heating bills; the bills for clothes and jewels and handbags; and the bills for groceries and sweets; for paintings and for tapestries; for fish and frogs with which to fill the moat; for stationery; for fresh flowers; for dry-cleaning; for redecorating; and for general amusement. And I haven't even gotten to the price of health insurance or the cost of unemployment or retirement plans.

With all this money going out, and not nearly as much of it coming in, the red castle began to run what we would call a deficit. It hadn't nearly as much money as it needed. And what little it had was flying out the door.

Which is why, one chilly evening in a drafty room, the red king found himself unhappily examining the ledger his accountant had just opened.

"What is this for?" he asked, pointing to a numbered line and frowning.

"Heraldry."

"What?"

"Flags and banners."

"Ah, yes," said the king. "A castle has to have those. Marketing and branding. Tell the world exactly who you are." His eyes moved down the page. "What's this?" he asked, pointing to another line.

"Er, pomp and circumstance," said the accountant, whose real name was Fred.

"Ah." The king pointed to a third line. "What about this?"

"Toiletries."

"What?"

"Toiletries." Fred cleared his throat. "Perfume, bath salts, hairspray, lipstick, shampoo, makeup, moisturizer, toenail polish…"

The king glared at him. "This is ridiculous," he spluttered.

"I've seen worse," said the accountant meekly.

"Who needs all of this?"

"The queen."

"The queen," the red king said after some thought, "is beautiful enough as is. The toiletries must go." He drew a fat red line through them.

Fred coughed. "The queen," he suggested humbly, "might not see this as you do."

"But I could buy a whole new set of golf clubs for this."

"And a cart. But not now," Fred hastened to add. "No more expenses. Not, at least, until you have some income—" which, for those of you too young to work, means money coming in.

The king sighed. He was very good at spending money. But the truth was, he wasn't nearly as good at making it. He had his taxes and his rents and one or two small jobs he did on the side. And, of course, he had his salary for being king. But it was clearly not enough.

Rouget, who had been listening outside the door, thought this might be the time to make his entrance. "Father," he said from across the room.

The king looked up and frowned. "What are you doing here?" he asked.

"I couldn't help but overhear what you were saying," said Rouget.

"That wasn't meant for you," the king snapped.

"But I want to help."

"Not now. We're working here."

"But I have an idea for you."

"We're very busy," said the king. "Why don't you run along."

Fred cleared his throat. "Perhaps," he suggested, studying his feet, "we ought to hear him out. One never knows."

"Oh, very well," the king sighed. "Go ahead."

Rouget meant to speak carefully. But all his words rushed out at once. "I've heard the blue castle has heaps of gold," he said, which wasn't strictly true but which undoubtedly strengthened his case.

"Indeed?" His father looked at him with interest.

"I have also heard," Rouget continued, more slowly this time, "the blue king, who has but a single daughter, would give much of it for her return. Should she go missing," he added, to be clear.

"A ransom," mused the king. "Now that's a thought. There hasn't been a kidnapping for ages."

Rouget thought it best not to correct him.

The king looked at Fred.

"It isn't a long-term solution," Fred said.

"Don't be such a party pooper." The red king remembered days when he was younger. Gleaming swords and midnight raids and maidens in distress. They were such good old days.

He turned back to his son. "Since you have clearly

given this some thought," he said, "might you have also thought about a plan?"

"Of course I have a plan," said Rouget, feeling very grown-up.

"Tell me," said the king.

And Rouget did.

The queen did not much like the plan. In fact, it might be fair to say she hated it.

"I won't," she said, when Rouget and his father asked her for her help. "I am a queen. I have my reputation to uphold."

"We wouldn't ask you if it weren't absolutely necessary," said the king.

"You don't need me," the queen said. "At least, not for this."

"Ah, but we do," the king replied.

"Why?"

The king turned to his son.

"The blue princess would never trust someone like me," said Rouget, skipping over *why* the princess wouldn't trust him—which, of course, had just a bit to do with having kidnapped her before.

"And you think she would trust your mother?"

"Wouldn't you?" asked Rouget sweetly.

"Most assuredly," the king said rather quickly.

"No," the queen insisted. "I won't do it." She was very stubborn.

The king sighed. He didn't like being heavy-handed. But he was a king, and he was used to having heavy hands. "Then I'm afraid we must discuss your toiletries," he said.

"My what?"

"Your doodads—perfume, nail polish, shampoo…" He listed them. "The truth is, we can no longer afford them."

The queen gasped. "But they're essential," she cried. The queen was a woman of a certain age, and toiletries were most important to her. "Do away with something else. A suit of armor. Or a golf bag. Not my toiletries. I need them."

"Look, dear," said the king, as patiently as possible. "We aren't getting rid of anything just yet. So long as you cooperate."

"But this is blackmail," cried the queen, which is a way of making someone do exactly as you wish.

"Why don't you think of it as teamwork?" said the king.

The queen glared. "Fine," she muttered, looking at her newly manicured nails. "When do we begin?"

"Tomorrow."

CHAPTER FOUR

The Ambush

Early the next day, the red king, the red queen, Rouget, Rojar, and two trusted servants set out for the blue castle which, as you already know, lay several kingdoms and one small mountain range away. Harold, when they had gone looking for him, had been nowhere to be found. "His loss," Rojar had said. And to be honest, they'd had a full party and he wasn't much missed. Which was really *their* loss. But we needn't dwell on this.

The queen complained the whole trip. She was, after all, a queen, and queens, as she let everybody know, were not supposed to be part of a raiding party. Queens stayed home, slept late, took long baths, tried on piles of designer clothes. They played cards, shopped for shoes, went to the hairdresser. They didn't head off long before the sun came up to steal a princess. And most certainly they didn't do it in a discount dress from several seasons back.

"You think she knows?" Rouget whispered to Rojar as he listened to his mother grumble.

"What, about that other kidnapping?"

"Yes."

"Did you say something?"

"No."

"Did she see something?"

"I don't think so."

"Then how would she know?"

Rouget shrugged. His mother always seemed to know things.

"Has she mentioned any missing toiletries?" Rojar had suddenly remembered several items that they hadn't yet returned.

"No."

"Not her bath salts?"

"Not even her second-favorite bathrobe."

Rojar nodded wisely. "Then I wouldn't worry."

The journey took much longer than Rouget remembered. At long last, the party spied Azula's castle in the distance. "Now remember," said the king, as the queen and the princes dug their hands into the dirt, "this is an ambush—" which means a surprise attack.

"I am aware of that," the queen muttered through gritted teeth. The dirt under her fingernails was horrible. Just horrible. She'd need a week of manicures to fix it. And a little something else to calm her nerves.

Now you may wonder why a queen and two red princes would go scrabbling in the dirt, when anyone could tell them that it's just as easy—if not easier—to carry out an ambush after having bathed. Indeed, some might even argue that it's better to be clean, as you and your activities are much less likely to be noticed. But Rouget's plan required dirt, as you shall shortly see.

"That's quite enough of that," the queen said, brushing off her hands.

"Don't brush them off," cried Rouget.

The queen glared at him. "This better work," she said.

"It will," said Rojar, who was wishing he had come up with the plan himself. It was a good plan—though not quite as good as his had been.

"Then let's get on with it," the queen said. "I, for one, would like to get this over with."

They made their way to the main gate and then inside. Almost at once, they came across a knight.

"Could you direct us to the gardens?" asked the queen in her best imitation of a servant's voice. She sounded nothing like a servant. Indeed, had the knight been listening more carefully, he might have said she sounded rather queenly.

But he didn't notice. For at heart, this knight was a poet, and he'd just composed a line of

RODERICK

53

poetry he rather liked and wanted to remember. "That way," he said, pointing to a narrow alley.

The queen curtsied stiffly. Then she elbowed Rouget and Rojar, who bowed.

And on they went.

They found the princess in the garden, reading a book.

"What a waste of time," said Rojar from behind a tree. He didn't much like books.

"A bore," Rouget agreed. He didn't like books either—which just goes to show what sort of princes they were.

"Gentlemen," their mother said. "We have an ambush waiting." For the record, she, too, didn't care for books.

The princes took a rose bush from a canvas sack.

Most roses, as I'm sure you know, are red. Some may be pink, and others may be yellow, and still others may be white, but when you close your eyes and think of roses, red is what you see. A deep, rich, satisfying red. And, not surprisingly, the red castle knew everything there was to know about red roses.

The blue castle, on the other hand, knew nothing. Zero. Zilch.

This was the key to Rouget's plan. And I am sorry to admit it was a good key.

He had seen Azula stare, astonished, at his mother's bath salts. He had seen the way she'd looked at the single carnation—red, of course—that he had given her, before she threw it at him. After she'd escaped, when he had tried and tried and tried—and failed—to come up with a new plan, he'd remembered how those looks had puzzled him. He'd thought about them 'til his head hurt. And he'd finally understood that something he thought common was, in fact, a thing of wonder. A red rose. It was so simple.

Rojar cut ten blossoms from the bush, and Rouget tied them with a velvet ribbon. Carefully, they trimmed the ends and sprayed the petals.

Then it was the queen's turn. Holding the bouquet in front of her, she walked across the garden, underneath the grape arbor and past the hedgerows trimmed to look like swans. When she was close enough to read the title of Azula's book, she stopped and cleared her throat.

The princess looked up with a start. She had been daydreaming of wide blue skies and lands outside the castle's walls.

"My lady," said the queen. The words did not come easily to her. But she did her best. "I've brought you roses."

"How unusual!" exclaimed the princess. She had never seen red roses.

"Yes," the queen agreed. "And very beautiful."

"Indeed." The princess reached out. "May I?"

"Certainly," the queen said. "Though you must beware the thorns."

Azula took the flowers.

"If you like them, I will plant a bush for you," the queen said, wiggling her fingers to display the dirt under her nails. "I am a gardener."

"I've never seen you here before," the princess said.

"No, I am new." The red queen watched Azula look the flowers over. "Smell them," she suggested. "They are fragrant as the summer."

"Truly?" asked Azula, and she smelled them.

The queen held her breath.

"That's odd," the princess said. And suddenly, she closed her eyes and fell asleep. You understand, of course: the roses had been sprayed with sleeping potion.

"Why, I've done it," said the queen, sounding surprised.

"Of course you have," cried Rouget as he ran out from behind a tree. He poked Azula to be sure she was asleep.

A moment later, the two servants wheeled the cart in.

"Quickly," said the king, and in a twinkling they deposited the princess in the bottom of the cart and carefully arranged some shrubbery around her.

"You were wonderful," the king said to the queen as the cart rolled along the path.

The queen looked pleased.

"It was *my* plan," said Rouget peevishly.

"And an exceedingly fine plan it was."

Rouget glanced in the cart, where he could just make out the outline of the sleeping princess. Once again, he had his prisoner. And this time, he'd make sure she married him.

The red king also looked down at their shrubby prize. He thought about the ransom he would ask for. One blue princess. She was worth a lot of gold.

CHAPTER FIVE

The Counselors

It did not take nearly as long, this time around, for the staff of the blue castle to notice Azula had gone missing; and this time, no one assumed that she was simply elsewhere. This time, the alarm went up at once. From then, it was but a simple matter to discover first the book, lying face down on the garden grass, then the cart tracks carved into the lawn, and then the knight who'd sent what he'd believed were gardeners to the garden.

"But they were wearing old clothes," said the knight, sounding distressed. "And they had dirty hands." He felt just awful. Here he was, a knight charged with protecting the blue castle. And he'd failed.

"It wasn't your fault," said the king, patting his arm. "There hasn't been a kidnapping for ages. These are peaceful times."

The knight, whose name was Roderick, nodded sadly. "Tell me," he said, "was it fearsome?"

"I'm afraid I wouldn't know," the king said. "But the garden was undamaged."

"And the princess?"

"Vanished."

"Let me rescue her," the knight said bravely.

"We have personnel for that."

"Please? It's the least that I can do."

The king took pity on the knight. "I'm gathering my counselors," he said. "You may sit in on the meeting."

"I'm most grateful," Roderick said and bowed.

The king called his staff together. "Gentlemen," he said.

The Lady Iris looked up. "I am not a gentleman."

"It was an expression," said the king. "You know what I meant."

"A king's words should be accurate." The Lady Iris was his older sister and could say what other people couldn't. "It is most important."

"Fine," the king said, feeling generous. "*Lady* and gentlemen."

The Lady Iris smiled.

"We have gathered to discuss important business," the blue king continued. He looked out over the audience before him. "The Princess Azula has been kidnapped."

There was silence.

"And we need to rescue her."

At once, the hall was filled with cheers.

"A princess rescue!" cried a young knight. "Capital!" He grabbed his sword and swished it through the air.

"Put that away!" thundered the justice minister, as the sword's point came dangerously near his hat.

"What are we waiting for?" another knight cried.

"Tally-ho!" shouted a third.

"All well and good," the minister of trade declared, crossing his arms. "But first we need to figure out—where is the princess? We can't rescue her if we can't find her."

"If my sister is correct," the king said, pointing at the Lady Iris, "the red castle is to blame."

"But how can you be sure?" demanded one of several wise men.

"Let me ask you something," said the Lady Iris. "If *you* were a kidnapper, and if *your* prisoner escaped, what would *you* do?"

"Consult my colleagues?"—who are other wise men—said the wise man.

"I'd go after her!" the young knight shouted.

"Hear, hear!" cried the other knights, thumping the floor.

The Lady Iris nodded knowingly. "Also," she added as the hall grew quiet, "there is this." Reaching in her pocket, she held up a red rose petal that Azula's maid had found beneath her book.

"What is it?" asked a wise man, shrinking back in horror.

"It's a petal. From a rose."

"It's hideous!" exclaimed the agriculture minister.

"It's horrible!"

"It is unnatural!"

"It is," the Lady Iris said, "proof."

"Blast the red castle!" an elder knight roared.

"Curse them!" cried the justice minister.

The knights all cheered.

The wise men also cheered.

"So tell me," said the minister of commerce, "how are we to go about the business of a princess rescue?"

"War," the minister of war said gravely.

"Hear, hear!" cried the knights again.

The blue king sighed. He was a peaceful king, and wanted to remain so. Wars could be unpleasant. And expensive, too. "There must be another way," he said, looking around.

The hall was silent.

"Someone must have an idea."

But it seemed no one did.

"Or a suggestion?"

Nothing.

"Anyone?"

After a moment, the knight Roderick raised his hand.

The other knights all turned to look at the newcomer.

"Yes?" the king said.

"I was wondering—" Roderick began.

The counselors shifted in their seats.

"Might it be possible—"

"Get on with it," said a mid-level wise man.

"I thought maybe—"

"Spit it out, son."

"Could we kidnap her?" said Roderick finally.

"Who?"

"The princess."

"She has already been kidnapped," the king pointed out.

"I mean kidnap her back."

"Outrageous," said the justice minister.

"Preposterous."

"Outlandish."

"Why? If they can steal her, so can we." Roderick was a young knight. And he didn't have a whole lot of experience. But being young and inexperienced meant he could think in bold and daring ways.

"It is absurd," said an old knight.

The blue king rubbed his beard. "It might work," he said thoughtfully.

"Your Majesty." The minister of war looked shocked.

The king ignored him. "It has possibilities," he said.

"I beg your pardon," said the minister, "but it has nothing of the sort."

"It's foolish," cried the education minister.

"Ridiculous."

"Think of your reputation."

"Think," the Lady Iris softly said, "of the Princess Azula."

"I am thinking of her," said the king. He looked at all the wise men and the counselors and the ministers and knights and the one lady, who looked back at him. "I have decided," he announced. "It is a fine plan. We will try it."

And, to Roderick's great surprise, they did.

As the king was making his decision, the Princess Azula awoke. She was in a covered wagon—not the gypsy wagon, which was bright and gay, and not the cart with shrubbery—but a drab wooden wagon with a hard bed and a slatted floor.

"Oh brother," she said. "Not again."

And though she knew she should be irritated or displeased, she wasn't. She'd spent weeks mooning about the castle, wishing for another grand adventure—or at least a little jaunt outside the castle's walls—and suddenly the very thing she'd wished for had come true. Let me be clear: she didn't like being a prisoner, or riding in a hard and bumpy wagon without so much as a toothbrush or a change of clothes. But it was exciting.

She peered through a knothole in the wagon's wall. Outside, the setting sun dipped low. The land turned pink and gold. Azula watched in wonder. She'd seen many wondrous things, of course; a princess always does. But they'd all been so civilized—which in this case means elegant and orderly: a fire in the great stone fireplace, the grape arbor after a storm, the hedgerows trimmed to look like swans.

The land under the sunset, on the other hand, was wild. Messy. Free. It filled her heart with happiness.

Then suddenly the wagon jolted to a stop. The window slot slid open and a face appeared. It was Rouget.

"Did you really think you could escape from me?" he said not-very-nicely.

"Is she up?" called a faint voice.

"Not quite," answered Rouget. He thrust his face close to the window. "We have captured you," he said triumphantly. "You are our prisoner again."

Azula sighed.

"Do you know what that means?"

"Rouget dear," the voice called.

"Just a minute, mother," said the red prince, sounding aggravated. Then he turned back to Azula. "It means you have to do what I tell you," he said. "And I'm telling you, you have to marry me."

"I told you last time," said Azula patiently. "I'll never marry you."

"Oh yes you will."

"No," said Azula. "Never."

"Don't be so sure," said Rouget unpleasantly. Glaring at his prisoner, he slammed the window panel shut—though not before he'd squirted in a puff of sleeping potion. Just to be mean.

"Oh you—" said Azula, but she was asleep before she'd finished saying what she'd meant to say.

And what was that? You scoundrel? Rascal? Termite? In fact, when she woke up later, what she said was peanut. Oh you peanut. Which seems just about right.

Rouget climbed back on his horse, and the red family continued homeward, across the sev-

68

eral kingdoms and the one small mountain range. The future looked bright. Here they had the open road before them and the princess locked up tight beside them. Soon, the king would have his ransom money and the queen her toiletries.

And, unbeknownst to both of them, the prince would have his bride.

"Hooray!" shouted Rouget. And no one disagreed.

CHAPTER SIX

The Escape

What the red king and queen and two princes couldn't possibly have imagined—although you and I, having excellent imaginations, might have—was that, having guessed with some accuracy the identity of the kidnappers, the blue castle had already sent a rescue party. Indeed, by the time the red party had slipped into its castle, climbed the stairs, and locked the prisoner in the southeast tower, Roderick and his men were but a day behind, and fast approaching.

You may wonder why the red king never thought to check his tracks. Most thieves—for that is what a kidnapper is—always keep one eye behind. But the red king was not a thief by nature, only by necessity—which meant he wasn't very skilled at thievery. Also, there was the small matter of the princes and their previous activities.

As you may recall, the red king and his wife had no

idea the princes had already tried their hand at kidnapping. And they had even less idea that this attempt at kidnapping had been successful. They assumed that when Azula disappeared from the blue castle, no one—and I mean absolutely no one—would know where to look for her. Accordingly, the king believed he had plenty of time in which to write a ransom note, hire an intermediary to deliver it, and have a glass of brandy in the meantime.

This was a mistake. And though it isn't very nice to take pleasure in others' misfortunes, I must say it pleases me immensely to report it. For this mistake helped level the playing field—which is a way of saying that at last the blue castle was not the only one being unpleasantly surprised.

But what of poor Azula locked up in the tower?

First, of course, she tried the door. It was locked—which, much to her relief, meant she could have a rescue.

Next she found the toy sword in the closet.

Finally, she flung open the window. "Can you hear me?" she called softly, hoping she might spy the dangling microphone. "Hello?"

But no one showed up at her door.

Sighing, she pulled up a chair and settled in. Surely, the masked man would come to rescue her. She wondered if he rescued other princesses, or only her, and hoped it wouldn't be a long wait for his services.

While Azula passed the night in sound sleep, dreaming of a rescue, Roderick and his men rode ever closer to the castle, until they could see it on

the far horizon, rising from the plains. Under the starry sky, they fed their horses, built a campfire, and toasted marshmallows before they crawled into their sleeping bags to dream courageous dreams.

In the morning, Roderick woke up feeling very brave. This is useful when your plans include a princess rescue.

"I am Roderick," he said proudly. "Knight of the blue castle."

"You might want to keep that to yourself," said one of his men, nodding towards the distant castle.

"Try again," the other man suggested.

Roderick cleared his throat. "I'm Roderick," he said boldly. Then, less boldly, "Poet."

"Lacks pizzazz," the first man said.

"I think it will do nicely," said the second man. "It's modest—" which essentially means lacking in pizzazz.

"A humble poet," Roderick said. "That's something I can work with." For in truth he was a poet, if not always humble.

As the sun began to rise above the trees, the poet Roderick walked around the campsite, practicing his poetry. In those days, people liked when poets read their poetry aloud. Quite frankly, I am sorry we do not do more of that ourselves. But I am also sorry that we rarely pause for tea, have lost the art of letter writing, and don't bother dressing up for dinner. But alas, so goes the world.

When Roderick finished with his recitations, the three knights had breakfast, packed up camp, and headed for their destination. It would be a long day's ride, but they would be outside the castle's walls by nightfall. And at last there'd be a princess rescue.

I t was at about this moment that Azula awoke, for princesses and knights keep very different schedules. "Today's the day I will be rescued," she sighed, thinking of the masked man—though she added, having manners, "Please."

No sooner had she spoken these words than there was a knock on the door.

"Yes?" she called out happily—for princesses, whose every wish is somebody's command, sometimes mistakenly believe that wanting something is the same as having it. She'd asked for a rescue and—presto!— here it was.

Except it wasn't.

The lock turned, the door opened, and there, in all his glory, stood Rouget.

"Oh brother," said Azula. "You again?" For she was greatly disappointed.

"Who were you expecting?"

"No one."

"Well then." Rouget dropped to one knee and held out a red rose. "Will you marry me?"

"What?"

"Will you marry me?" he said impatiently.

"Of course not," said Azula. "I've already told you that."

"Don't you have any manners?" Rouget asked her crossly. "When a prince asks you to marry him, the only thing to say is yes."

"But I don't want to marry you," Azula said.

Rouget got to his feet. "The way I see it," he said irritably, "you don't have a choice. I only asked you to be nice." He scowled at her. "You're going to marry me. In fact, you're going to marry me tomorrow. And there's nothing you can do about it." Flinging the rose to the floor, he stomped out, making sure to lock the door and take the key.

Azula stared at the locked door. Tomorrow? That left almost no time. What if it took two days for the masked man to arrive?

She hurried to the window. "Please," she whispered, looking out, "come rescue me."

But no one came.

The morning passed.

The afternoon passed.

And then it was night.

Sitting at the window, staring at the moon, Azula felt the tears well in her eyes. Would no one save her? Would she really have to marry Rouget? It was too terrible to think about. Unhappy and alone, she lay her head against the window sill and cried.

But what Azula didn't know was that all afternoon, her would-be rescuer had been extremely busy. I don't mean the brave knight Roderick who, as you remember, had his own plan to attend to. I am talking here of Harold.

Harold had been well aware of the activities in the red castle's southeast tower. He had seen his brothers' comings and their goings; and he'd noticed, as he'd tiptoed past the sixth-floor prison, that the key was missing from its lock. All afternoon, as Rouget had his hair trimmed and his clothes pressed and his shoes shined, Harold had been searching for a copy of the key. It took a long time. But he'd found one, at last, on a large ring in the back of the main office, where the castle's manager stored all the spare keys.

Carefully, he'd pocketed it. But then he'd had to wait. And wait. And wait until the castle's occupants had had their dinner and their baths, and brushed their teeth, and settled down to sleep. And then he'd had to wait until they *were* asleep. Indeed, it was half past midnight when he finally climbed the stairs and quietly slipped down the hall and through the secret passage.

Standing in the dark, he fastened his mask. Then he slid the extra key into the lock and opened it.

Azula looked up from the window sill. Her spirits lifted and her eyes grew bright. "You've come!" she said, sounding relieved.

The masked man looked at her with some surprise. He'd been expecting someone new. "But I already rescued you," he stammered.

"Yes," Azula said. "I'm sorry."

"It's alright," said Harold. "I don't mind." He didn't, either.

There was a long pause.

"Well, do you want another rescue?" he asked after several awkward moments.

"Yes," Azula answered promptly. "Please."

"I'll have to come up with a plan." And Harold sat down on the bed to think.

"I don't mean to be rude," Azula interrupted him. "But could you think of this plan quickly?"

"Why the hurry?"

"Because," she said with a tremor in her voice, "the prince intends to marry me. Tomorrow."

"It is after midnight," said the masked man. "It is already tomorrow."

"Then there isn't any time."

"We have all night," said Harold, who was well aware how very late his brother slept. He stood up from the bed. "I need to make a few arrangements," he continued. "Sit tight. I'll be back."

But it is difficult to sit tight when the red prince several towers over has been dreaming of a wedding you would rather not have. By the time Harold returned, Azula was more than a little anxious. And you can't blame her for that.

Breathing hard, the masked man dropped a bundle on the bed.

"What is that?" asked Azula.

"Your disguise." The masked man looked quite pleased.

The blue princess unwrapped the bundle. Inside was a red knight's uniform.

"It was the smallest I could find," the masked man said apologetically. "But it should do."

"I can't wear this." Azula, I am sorry to say, sounded horrified.

"Why not?"

"It is a knight's uniform."

"Indeed."

"I am a princess."

But the masked man didn't seem to understand.

"A princess doesn't wear this sort of thing," Azula said. "A princess wears—" she shrugged; how to explain it?—"princess clothes." Without those clothes—without the perfect fit and the fine fabric—she would be quite ordinary. And the masked man made her wish to be extraordinary.

"Would you rather wear a wedding dress?"

She shook her head.

"Then you will have to wear this uniform. I cannot rescue you in that." The masked man pointed to her blue dress.

And, of course, Azula wanted to be rescued. So she did what any reasonable princess would: she wore the uniform.

The clothes were much too big, of course. Azula rolled the pants and sleeves up. Then she turned in a slow circle. "Well?" she asked.

The masked man eyed her critically. "You are the nicest looking knight I've ever seen," he said.

Azula blushed.

"But never mind. It's late. It's dark. No one will look too closely."

He adjusted one of her cuffs. "There. That's better. Now you're good to go."

Azula's heart beat faster.

"Take the secret stairway through the southeast tower, like we did the last time," the masked man continued. "At the gate, the guard will say, 'What ho?' and you have to say, 'Hail!' Then—"

"Wait," Azula interrupted him. "You aren't coming?"

Harold shook his head. "I can't. Not this time." What he didn't say was that Rouget had posted several guards, and he'd most certainly be recognized.

"Without a rescuer, it won't be a real rescue," said Azula.

"It will be a real escape," said Harold. "Which is just as good." He handed her a compass. "When you leave the castle, head northeast about two miles. You'll find three knights waiting for you by a campfire." Harold had seen them through his telescope.

"I'm sorry you're not coming," said Azula.

"Me, too," said the masked man. And he was.

Impulsively, which means without thinking too much, Azula kissed him. This was most unusual, for ordinary princesses are very cautious about whom they kiss. But Azula was already starting to become a much more interesting kind of princess. "Thank you," she said, stepping back.

Beneath his mask, the masked man blushed. "It was my pleasure," he said honestly. "Now off you go. And try not to come back."

CHAPTER SEVEN

The Disguise

zula's escape went just as planned. She took the secret passage to the secret stairway to the secret exit. At the door, the red guard barely glanced up from his paper.

"What ho?" he said, sounding bored.

"Hail!" she answered boldly, and without another look, he waved her through. It was that easy.

Outside the castle walls, a soft wind blew in from the east where, far away, Azula's home awaited her. The night air smelled like apples. Overhead, the sky glittered with stars. Wearing the ill-fitting uniform, and with the toy sword belted to her side, Azula didn't look much like a princess. And to tell the truth, she didn't feel much like one either. But she felt something unusual.

She felt free.

And, with some surprise, she realized she liked this feeling.

Gently, she drew out the compass. On its cover were the letters RPH. Now you and I both know—or should know with some little thought—that these initials stand for Royal Prince Harold. But Azula didn't know this. She knew Harold only as the masked man—which was not much of a name at all.

RPH, however, almost spelled the name Ralph. She would call the masked man Ralph. It was a pleasant name, and seemed somehow to suit him.

So with Ralph's name in her thoughts, and his compass in her hand, she headed, as she'd been instructed, northeast.

Princesses, unfortunately, aren't used to walking very far. And two miles, for those of you who've never walked it, is a fair way—more than fair if all you wear are dainty shoes and satin slippers. In her past life, the Princess Azula, who'd never so much as owned a pair of sneakers, would have called for a cab. Or a carriage. Or a horse, at least. But out under the starry sky, beyond the glow cast from the castle's lights, there wasn't anyone to call. Azula was entirely—and I mean absolutely—on her own.

Was she scared? I would certainly have been so: kidnappers behind me and the great unknown before me. But Azula was adventurous of spirit. She had never understood this because princesses are not allowed to be adventurous. But surely some of them  are, just like some of us must be. It simply takes the proper situation to discover it.

Guided by the small beam of a flashlight she'd found in her pocket, Azula made her way across the darkened countryside. She walked and walked and walked and walked, on rocky paths and through high grasses, over small hills and across fields filled with wildflowers. And at last she saw, as Ralph had said she would, the red glow of a campfire.

"Who goes there?" cried a harsh voice.

"Who is asking?" she said.

In reply, she saw the flash of silver swords.

"It is a red knight," someone whispered.

"Sir, throw down your weapon," the harsh voice commanded.

"But I haven't got one," said Azula.

"Sir," the voice continued. "Do you think we jest? Your sword. Please."

Azula put her hand to her side. There, indeed, she found a sword. "Oh, it is but a toy," she said, placing the toy sword on the ground.

"How very strange," the voice said. For the red knight didn't sound much like a knight. "Who are you?"

Azula hesitated.

"Sir." A sword gleamed in the firelight.

"I am Azula," said Azula.

There was a small gasp, and three knights stepped out of the shadows.

"Can it be?" The tallest of the three came forward. Then he bowed.

"Why, this is most extraordinary," he said. "My sincere apologies."

Azula nodded graciously.

"But in those clothes—" the blue knight gestured at the uniform—"I simply couldn't tell. Forgive me, but you don't look like a princess."

"You don't have to rub it in," Azula muttered, though she wondered why it mattered. You see: she was learning.

The man bowed again. "I am the blue knight Roderick," he said. "Come to rescue you."

Azula curtsied. "Thank you," she said. "But as you can see, I've already escaped."

"Had you no help?"

"I had a rescuer," she said.

The blue knight tried to hide his disappointment. Here he'd traveled across several kingdoms and one mountain range, and someone else had done his job. "Where is he?" he demanded, peering cautiously into the shadows.

"He had to remain behind," Azula answered, with a small pang of regret.

"Your rescuer abandoned you?" The knight looked shocked.

"No," she said quickly. "He had—" she paused— "other obligations."

Roderick looked at her with disapproval. "This is most irregular," he said.

"Is it?"

"A rescuer abandoning a princess? How is he supposed to be your champion if he sends you off alone? The world is full of dangers. You need a protector." Roderick pursed his lips and thought a moment. "There must be another way," he muttered.

Frowning, he paced back and forth before the princess. "Ah!" he suddenly exclaimed. "I have it! Maybe *I* could step in."

"You?" Azula said.

"It's very untraditional—this coming in after the rescue. But it might be done." The knight looked at the princess. "That is, if you'll have me."

"Certainly," Azula said—for what choice did she have?

"I am most honored," Roderick said and bowed again.

Azula thought of the old horse, the ride across the countryside, the steam train and, of course, the masked man. Then she put those thoughts aside. This was to be a different kind of rescue.

"We must leave at once," said Roderick. "Your escape is sure to be discovered." He paused. "First, however, there's the matter of this uniform. It's not the least bit suitable for you." He circled her, examining the clothes distastefully. "Although—" he stopped abruptly as a new plan suddenly occurred to him— "why, yes, I should think they'd suit *me* very nicely."

"You?" Azula said.

"Indeed."

"Then what shall *I* wear?"

Roderick sighed. "There is no choice," he said. "You'll have to wear these." And he pointed to his own clothes.

Now, if you have ever worn a shirt for more than two days and, on top of that, if you have ever ridden across several kingdoms and one mountain range wearing that shirt, you'll understand how very unpleasant this proposition was—in other words, it stunk.

But Roderick was insistent. And because he was a blue knight, and because he'd ridden all this way to rescue her, Azula did as she was told. Arrangements were made; clothes exchanged. Roderick the blue knight walked off into the woods; and Roderick the red knight emerged.

"Whyever do you want to be a red knight?" asked Azula, trying not to breathe too deeply.

"It is the best way to get inside the castle," Roderick said, forgetting he'd just offered to escort her home.

Azula looked at him in wonder. "You mean to go back there?"

"I will find out what their plan is." Roderick's princess rescue had been thwarted. But a knight was still a knight.

"Won't that be dangerous?"

"Of course," said Roderick happily. And taking up his sword, he bid the princess and his men farewell and set off through the dark.

CHAPTER EIGHT

The Spy

Inside the red castle, there was much hand-wringing once it was discovered that the prisoner had vanished.

"This is dreadful!" cried the red king. "What are we to do?"

"Do?" said the queen. "We'll do what we have always done." And off she swept to use her toiletries—while she still had them.

The king called his sons together.

"Gentlemen," he said, for kings are often very formal with their sons. "We have a problem."

His sons looked at him expectantly.

"The princess has gone missing."

"Missing?" gasped Rouget. He wondered if he'd left the door unlocked.

"What princess?" Harold asked quite cleverly. Because of course he knew about the princess. Indeed, he

knew more than anyone about her. But he didn't have to say so.

"The princess we kidnapped," said his father.

"You kidnapped a princess?" Harold's cheeks glowed. Just the mention of Azula made his heart beat faster. It's amazing what one kiss can do.

"We had a fine adventure," said the king. "Your mother was tremendous."

"It was *my* idea," muttered Rouget.

"An excellent idea, too," said his father.

"Why would *you* kidnap a princess?" Harold asked Rouget.

"To marry her."

"To what?" It was their father's turn to look surprised.

Rouget shrugged. "I'm a prince," he said by way of explanation.

"But that princess was for ransoming." The king frowned. "Not for marrying."

"Right now she's not for either," Rojar pointed out.

"Ah, yes." The king looked chastened, which means he'd just been reminded that the princess—and his ransom—had both vanished. "So then let me get straight to the point: we must be on our guard."

"You think her castle will attack?" asked Rouget eagerly.

"One never knows," the king replied.

"Hooray!" cried Rojar. "Man the battlements!"

The king imagined clashing swords and flying flags and maidens in distress. His bad knee hurt and his back ached. Perhaps the good old days were not so good as he remembered. "Not so fast," he said. "We're not under attack just yet."

"We will be soon," said Rojar optimistically.

The king had to agree. "I think we must prepare," he said reluctantly. "Perhaps it's time to call a meeting of the senior staff."

He summoned his two messengers.

"Your wish is our command," they cried in unison. And bowing low, they went to sound their trumpets and to spread the word before the blue castle could make its move.

As you and I both know, however, the blue castle had already sprung into action. While the messengers blew their trumpets and the red king scribbled out a speech, the brave knight Roderick wandered through the unfamiliar castle, taking notes and drawing maps and trying to blend in. This was much easier than he'd imagined; indeed, it turned out to be a snap.

For once you have become a knight in one castle you may, with but a few adjustments, be a knight in any castle. I suppose it is like being a cook: once you've learned the recipes, it doesn't make much difference whose kitchen you're in. Roderick the blue knight was simply in a different kitchen; all he needed was to find out where the salt was kept, and where the sugar.

But the red castle was bigger than the blue castle. A single knight, much like a tourist in a foreign country, would need many days to properly explore. Roderick did the best he could. But he'd already traveled across several kingdoms and one mountain range. And he was tired. What he really wanted was to sit and put his feet up. So he did what any tourist might: he found a park and bought an ice cream. Strawberry.

What Roderick didn't know was that this was no ordinary park. It was a garden. More precisely, it was the red castle's rose garden, and it was filled with blooming roses. Crimson roses, scarlet roses, ruby, cherry, fuchsia roses; every shade of red you could imagine. It was quite extraordinary.

But the brave knight Roderick was a blue knight. And he was a blue knight who was far from his home. Sitting on the park bench eating ice cream he wished, more than anything, to see a morning glory or a hyacinth or a hydrangea—which are all blue flowers, and which just might make him feel less homesick. All that red. It was a little overwhelming.

Looking at the field of flowers, he let out a heartfelt sigh.

"Why so sad?" a gentle voice asked.

Roderick jumped. Before him stood a lovely maiden with a garden trowel.

"I am thinking of my home," he answered.

"Is this not your home?"

Although his current mission may have made him seem dishonest, Roderick was an honest knight. All good knights are—at least that is their reputation. "No," he said. "I come from far away. I'm here on business."

"I am glad for that." The maiden smiled.

Roderick noticed that her lips were very red. Like roses. But her eyes were blue. A cool, clear, swimming-pool blue. Suddenly, he felt less homesick. "I also am glad," he said.

Again, the maiden smiled. This time Roderick noticed that her teeth were very white.

Just then there was the sound of trumpets.

"Hear ye, hear ye," cried a messenger. He cleared his throat; the shouting made him hoarse. "A meeting of the senior knights is called. The senior knights. No junior knights. No middle management. Report at once. That's all." And off he hurried, spreading the king's proclamation.

Roderick turned back to the maiden. He had just recalled a line of poetry he wanted to recite.

BRONWYN

"Might that be you?" the maiden asked. "A senior knight?"

The blue knight Roderick started. He had clean forgotten he was dressed as a red knight. "Oh yes, indeed it is," he said quite hastily. "Forgive me. I must go. Although," he added, gazing into her blue eyes, "I'd much prefer to stay."

"As I, too, would prefer you did." The maiden blushed.

Beside the bench he sat on, Roderick spied a rose bush. Gallantly, he plucked a flower.

"Ouch!" he cried. The rose's thorn had done its job.

"Oh, you are wounded," cried the maiden as a small trickle of blood appeared.

"It's nothing," Roderick said.

"Does it hurt terribly?"

"No, it is but a scratch."

"Sir, you are very brave." The maiden handed him a band-aid.

Roderick bowed. "My thanks," he said, wrapping his finger. "You have been a great comfort to me. But duty calls—" which means he had a meeting to attend.

He started off, but quickly spun around. "Your name," he called to her. "What is your name?"

For names, in stories as in life, are crucial. Have you ever had a friend whose name you didn't know? Or been told a story in which interesting characters went nameless? Nor have I. So listen closely.

"Bronwyn," said the maiden.

Now we may be sure to hear of her again.

"Bronwyn," repeated Roderick. And because she was a maiden, and because all knights need maidens—blue or red or in distress or otherwise—he made sure to remember it.

CHAPTER NINE

The Meetings

The senior knights met in a medium-sized conference room in the north tower of the west wing. Roderick, as expected, wasn't on the guest list. But he had discovered something useful in his wandering about the castle: if you walked like a red knight, and talked like a red knight and, most important, dressed like a red knight, then people would assume you *were* a red knight—even if you weren't.

"Sorry," said the knight taking attendance. "But you aren't on my list."

"There must be some mistake," said Roderick.

"No mistake," the man said. "Look—you aren't here." He waved his clipboard in the air.

"But I'm a senior knight."

"You'll have to take that up with management." The knight turned to the next person in line.

"See here." Roderick drew himself up tall. "I am a senior knight, and I'm expected at this meeting. If my name's not on your list, then put it there." He was impressive, if a little pushy. For like many knights, he understood the value of a thing we grown-ups call self-confidence—which means if you believe in yourself, so will others.

"But—"

"Give me a pen; I'll write it in myself."

"But this is never done."

"Would you prefer I use my weapon?"

"No." The red knight looked alarmed. "That won't be necessary. Go on in."

Nodding his thanks, the blue knight Roderick went into the meeting.

It was a most interesting meeting.

First, a red knight called the room to order. Then another red knight made some introductory remarks. And then, at last, the red king stood and spoke.

"Gentlemen," he said, looking around. There weren't any ladies. "I have summoned you because we have—in short, we have a problem."

A wave of excitement swept the room.

"We have been warned, through unofficial channels, that a distant castle has been planning an attack." This wasn't strictly true, of course. But it got everyone's attention—which had been the point.

"What?" cried a skinny knight with flowing moustaches. "Whoever would attack *us*?"

The king cleared his throat. "I wouldn't like to say just yet," he said. "But if you must know, it is the blue castle."

Roderick gasped. He knew this was a lie.

"How dare they?" roared the knight.

"The insolence."

"The nerve."

"What have we ever done to them?"

The red king coughed. Because, of course, there was the tiny matter of the kidnapping. Which he did not intend to mention. "I am telling this to you," he said, "because we need to be prepared."

"We don't need to prepare," the knight with the long moustaches declared. "We need to strike."

"Hear, hear," cried a small handful of the junior senior knights.

The senior senior knights were more restrained. "There must be other options," one with bushy eyebrows said.

The king agreed. A castle attack could be disagreeable. And time-consuming. Not to mention dangerous and, worst of all, expensive. He would much rather work on his golf game. Or go out to dinner. Or, perhaps, both.

"Maybe we could send a delegation," one knight said. "To—you know—talk things over."

"No."

"Form a committee?"

"No."

"What if we kidnapped someone?" said the knight with bushy eyebrows.

"Like who?"

"Don't they have a princess?"

"Yes, indeed they do."

"Well then, let's kidnap her."

"Oh, splendid."

"Wonderful."

"Magnificent."

The knights all cheered. There hadn't—they thought—been a kidnapping for ages. And what better way to launch the first strike?

The king looked around the room with satisfaction. It had been a most successful meeting. His knights had been admirable. Humming cheerfully under his breath, he smiled. He would get his ransom yet.

And Roderick? As the red knights filed from the conference room, the blue knight wondered how he could get word back to his castle that the princess was, again, in danger.

Let us, for the moment, leave the brave knight Roderick and return to the blue castle, where the princess and her two escorts were just arriving, looking like they all could use a good meal and a bar of soap.

They wound their way along the streets, their horses' hooves clop-clopping on the cobblestones. And here is what Azula found most interesting: nobody recognized her. Sure, the sun was setting and the shadows lengthening. But more significantly, she was wearing Roderick's unwashed—and by this time rather icky—clothes, and not the fine dress and the sparkling jewels the castle was accustomed to. And this made all the difference.

"Oh, good heavens!" cried the castle's housekeeper when the bedraggled princess showed up at the door. "What happened?" And looking, I am sorry to say,

most embarrassed, she hustled the princess to a bath before she might be glimpsed by anybody else.

Azula herself wasn't in the least ashamed. Not all that long ago she might have been; indeed, you may recall her hesitation when the masked man handed her the getaway clothes. But the princess had learned many lessons lately, one of which was that life on the open road is easier without a suitcase and in pants. Sitting in her bubble bath, Azula thought of her escape across the several kingdoms and the one small mountain range, and wondered how she ever might have managed in a dress.

And was she any less a princess for it?

No. Of course not.

Even with her tangled hair and ragged nails and dirty smudges on her face; even wearing Roderick's clothes, without a jewel in sight, she was the blue Princess Azula.

But—who was this princess?

For the princess who returned to the blue castle was far different from the one who'd left. Everything about her old life bored her now: the clothes, the dinners and desserts, even the books all paled when held against the thrill of her adventures. Walking round the hedges shaped like swans—which once had seemed so beautiful—she'd think about the crackling campfire, the wide and starry sky that spread above her while she slept, the masked man—always the masked man—and she'd begin to feel the walls of the blue castle close about her like a prison. It was that bad. Sometimes she would hold the compass in her hand, letting its little arrow sway and wondering what lay in each direction. Once in a great while she would even wish that someone from the north or south might come and carry her off—just for a few days, just long enough to feel the wind in her hair and the road beneath her feet.

But no one came, for this was not that sort of rescue. If Azula needed rescuing this time, the only one to do it was Azula.

So it was that soon thereafter, when the blue king gathered his counselors together, Azula insisted he include her. After all, the subject of the meeting was the red castle and who better than she to give advice?

"Why, this is unheard of," said the king in consternation. His daughter was supposed to shop and go to parties. Maybe cut some ribbons, or kiss babies. Not participate in international relations.

"But I know more about the red castle than anyone," Azula said.

"My dear," the king continued, not unkindly, "we have scholars studying the castle. We have policy advisors looking at its policies, and military strategists examining its military. In short, we have experts of all sorts."

"But they have never been inside."

The king could not deny this.

"I have walked the secret passageway," Azula said. "I've said the secret password. I have even—" she paused, for she'd suddenly remembered something—"I have even watched the brave knight Roderick turn into a spy."

"You don't say," said the king. "However did he do it?"

But Azula didn't answer. "Take me to your meeting," she said. "I will tell you everything."

"By all means," said the king. "Let us go in."

It took but several minutes for the counselors to decide they had to contact Roderick. Unfortunately, castles of the time did not have telephones; smoke signals were impractical; homing pigeons unreliable; and sending anything by post was hopeless.

"We'll have to dispatch a scout," the king declared.

His counselors agreed.

"But who?"

Several knights held up their hands. They were sorry they had scoffed at Roderick's plan. For now, while he was being brave and knightly, wearing a red uniform and rubbing elbows with the enemy and who knows what else, they were stuck inside a meeting. And on such a nice day, too.

"Our scout must be bold," a senior counselor said. "Courageous. Daring."

"And he must be clever."

"Trustworthy."

"Resourceful."

The counselors looked around the room at all the

eligible—which, in this case, means the bold, courageous, daring, clever, trustworthy, resourceful—knights.

"Whom shall we choose?" asked the king. It was a very difficult decision. Carefully, he studied the selection. "It is not an easy choice," he murmured. "We have many fine men."

The knights shifted in their seats.

"It is a dangerous job," he went on. "But most important. Maybe we should…"

"I will go," Azula said.

"What?"

"I will go."

The knights looked ill. The counselors looked horrified. "But you aren't the least bit qualified," one finally spluttered.

"But I am," Azula said. "I'm bold. Courageous. Daring. Clever. Trustworthy. Resourceful. And more than that, I've been inside the castle. Twice. I am experienced."

The king was flustered. This was not the daughter he had raised. "A princess doesn't do this sort of thing," he said.

"This princess does."

The Lady Iris smiled.

And what choice did the king have?

Roderick's clothes were washed and altered, food was packed, an escort chosen, and after a good night's sleep, Azula set off for the distant kingdom, looking poised and proud upon her horse.

CHAPTER TEN

The Maid

The journey back to the red castle seemed much shorter than the journey out. This often is the case—perhaps because the route becomes familiar. In no time at all, Azula and her escorts found themselves in the red kingdom, making camp beside a grove of redwood trees. They boiled water for hot

cocoa, toasted marshmallows, and told each other scary stories about sleeping potions, gypsy wagons, prisoners, and spoiled princes.

Late that night, Azula lay inside her sleeping bag beside the fire, staring at the starry sky above. The world was a big place—big and exciting—and it held adventures by the handful. She just had to find them.

Reaching in her pocket, she touched Ralph's golden compass. So many different directions. Which one would be hers? And would it lead to him? She took a deep breath and the night air smelled like smoke and chocolate and the world felt full of possibilities. She watched the stars above her wink and glitter. Then she closed her eyes and dreamed of lands she'd never seen, and people she had not yet met.

In the morning, Azula changed into the maid's dress she had saved from her first rescue. This time she did not complain, for she no longer minded. She packed a sand-wich, pet her horse, and bid her two escorts farewell. They weren't at all pleased; being left behind was not the least bit knightly. But the red castle, surely, would be on the lookout for knights.

And indeed it was. There were archers on the castle's roof and guards at the main gate; security patrols; metal detectors; undercover agents; even one red knight working a polygraph machine, which is a lie detector. Every possible precaution had been taken to weed out unwanted knights.

But Azula was no knight. She was a maid. And no one cared about a kitchen maid.

She waited on line; had her satchel x-rayed; passed beneath the stern inspection of the sentries at the drawbridge; and, at last, she made her way inside.

Now it was time to find the brave knight Roderick in his red knight uniform.

She found him on a park bench, scribbling in a note-book with a quill—a feather—pen. The feather had been taken from a handsome, if unpleasant, swan. Don't ever do this. Swans are mean and don't like having feathers plucked—though you yourself might also hiss if someone pulled a handful of your hair to make a pen, however beautiful.

Roderick sighed and scribbled. Then he scratched out several words, sighed once again, and scribbled several more.

"What are you writing?" asked Azula.

Roderick jumped. He'd thought himself alone.

"It is a poem," he said. "To a lady. I am looking for a word that rhymes with heart."

"Smart," said Azula promptly.

Roderick shook his head. "Too snappy. I need longing. Sorrow. Courage. Pain." He touched the band-aid on his hand.

Azula thought a moment. "How about apart?" she asked.

"Apart," repeated Roderick slowly. Then he said

the word again. "Why yes, that's it exactly. Thank
you." And he wrote it down.

"Do you miss her most dreadfully?" Azula asked
him, feeling flattered.

"Not yet," said the knight. "Though such a time
may come." He gave the kitchen maid—for that is
what she seemed to him—a closer look. "But who are
you to ask such questions?"

The Princess Azula leaned in close. "I am Azula of the blue castle," she whispered. "Don't you recognize me?"

Roderick gave a start. For now that she mentioned it, she did look rather like Azula.

"But...I...you..." he spluttered. "But what happened? You look terrible." He gestured at the maid's dress. True, the last time he had seen her she was wearing knight's clothes. But at least he'd been the knight whose clothes they were.

"I have disguised myself," Azula answered proudly. "For my job."

"Your job?" Roderick looked horrified. "A princess doesn't have a job. Unless," he reconsidered, "it is to be a princess."

Azula sighed. "I am a scout," she patiently explained. "I've come to take your news back to the castle."

"You?"

"Yes."

"But it cannot be." Although he was a young knight, Roderick was conventional—which means he didn't much like change.

"And yet it is," Azula answered.

Roderick frowned. "I cannot go along with this," he said. "It's inappropriate—" which means it ought not to be done. "And dangerous," he added, almost as an afterthought.

"Then what do you propose?"

"Send someone else," he answered instantly.

"There isn't anyone."

"There must be." Roderick looked around.

"There's only me," Azula said. "What is your news?"

The brave knight Roderick hesitated. He would have to do something he'd never done before: namely, change his beliefs. That takes a kind of courage, too.

"Sir," said Azula. "I am waiting for your news. By order of the king."

And how could Roderick now object? He couldn't. Call it progress.

"Very well." The knight leaned in and lowered his voice. "The red castle has a new plan."

"Truly?" Azula felt a shiver of excitement. "What is it?"

Roderick made sure there was no one listening. "The red king intends to kidnap…" The knight looked uncomfortable. "The thing is," he continued hesitantly, "he intends to kidnap *you*."

"He does?" Azula would have thought two kidnappings were plenty.

"Yes," the knight said, brightening. For he had had a sudden revelation. "Which means we must get you out of here." He sprang up from the bench. At last. A princess rescue. "Come," he said delightedly, "let us be off." He offered her his arm.

And though Azula could have told him she was capable of walking out herself, she didn't. Sometimes it's best to let a knight feel knightly.

N ow, at last, we come to the part of the story where things don't go as planned. It happens. You put on a shirt you had been saving for a special day, only to find it is too small; or else you try to make banana sandwiches for your tea party, only to discover somebody has eaten all the fruit. And what is there to do but be quick-witted and good-natured?

Roderick and Azula headed for the castle's gate. "Act natural," the blue knight whispered. This is easy for a knight dressed as a knight; less easy for a princess masquerading as a maid. A princess is a princess through and through. But then, what maid is not a princess inside, too?

Azula held her head high as she walked beside the knight. Her steps were bold. Her eyes were bright.

And people noticed.

"You!"

Azula didn't pay attention. No one ever talked to her that way.

"You there!"

But someone, indeed, was addressing her. She turned to find the head housekeeper beckoning.

"What is this?" asked the head housekeeper. "There's no romance on the job."

"But I pine for another," Roderick said.

"You do?" Azula looked at him with some surprise.

The head housekeeper frowned. "You knights are all the same," she said, sounding exasperated. "Go on. Shoo." She waved her hands at Roderick, who had the good sense to slink away—though not, as you shall soon see, very far. "And as for you," she said, taking Azula by the arm, "you come along. There's work to do." Keeping a firm grip on her kitchen maid, she whisked the princess through the door.

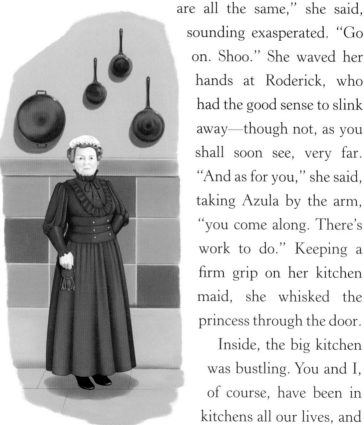

Inside, the big kitchen was bustling. You and I, of course, have been in kitchens all our lives, and

if you are like me, you think them rather ordinary. But Azula, who had never been inside a kitchen, found it fascinating. There were plates and pots and cups and platters; pitchers, peelers, mixers, mashers. And the food! Think of whatever you might like for tea—for it was time for tea—and triple it: croissants and cookies; bread and jam; hot scones and dainty finger sandwiches; and candied orange slices, chocolate truffles, layered cakes, raspberry tarts. Azula, who had never thought to ask how food was cooked, was mesmerized. She stood and stared.

"What are you staring at?" the sous-chef asked.

"You'd think she'd never been inside a kitchen," his assistant scoffed.

"You there." A cook in a white apron thrust a tray of cookies into her hands. "Take these upstairs."

"Who, me?" Azula blanched.

"Of course you," snapped the cook.

Azula didn't want to go upstairs. Upstairs was the

red king. The red queen. And worst of all, the two red princes.

"Go," the cook said, pointing to the stairs and glaring. "Now."

And what else could Azula do? Holding the tray, she slowly climbed the stairs.

CHAPTER ELEVEN

The Discovery

For a castle, the blue castle was a simple place. Not so the red castle. Azula looked around in awe. The dining room was splendid; the red queen had seen to that. Indeed, she had redecorated several times—which made her decorator very happy, and a little richer, too.

Azula set the tray of cookies on the table.

"Bring that over here." Waving a painted fingernail, the red queen didn't even look up from her fashion magazine. Azula wondered what could be so interesting about a bunch of clothes. Then she remembered that she, too, had once found such things fascinating.

The red queen groped for a cookie. Her rings glinted in the light.

"Your tea is served," the butler said.

Azula thought it a fine time to leave. She turned to go just as Prince Harold entered.

Harold gasped. Azula, as you may recall, had no idea who Harold was without his mask. But Harold knew exactly who Azula was. And you can very well imagine his surprise when he found that the princess he had rescued—twice—was serving him his tea.

Now this is where the story gets exciting.

For behind Prince Harold were the other two red princes, Rouget and Rojar. And naturally, when Harold started both looked to see why.

"It's just a kitchen maid," said Rouget, heading for the plate of cookies. He particularly liked the ones with jam.

"She is a pretty maid," said Rojar cautiously.

"But still a maid." Rouget believed a prince should

never mingle with a maid—which only goes to show how silly this prince was. For some maids are quite fine, just as some princes aren't.

"Harold seems to like her," said Rojar. For it was true—Harold was staring at the maid.

"He hasn't any sense."

Rojar agreed. "And yet—" he squinted at the maid—"she seems somehow familiar."

"Nonsense."

"But she does."

It was at this point that Azula tried to slip out of the room.

"One minute," said the queen. "You haven't poured my tea." She looked up from her fashion magazine to see the maid who'd been remiss—which means who hadn't done her job.

And what did she see instead?

"My toiletries!" she shrieked.

The princes looked at her.

"I beg your pardon?" said Rouget.

"My perfumes! My shampoos! My nail polish!" For I am sorry to report that what the queen saw wasn't the blue princess or, indeed, even a prisoner on the loose. It was the ransom money.

"Mother?" said Rojar. "Are you all right?"

The king came running. "What is it, my dear?" he asked.

"It's her!" the queen shrieked, pointing at Azula.

"Who?"

The red queen shook her finger.

"She is but a maid," the king said as Azula, still holding the teapot, backed against the wall. "Look at those clothes."

"It's the blue princess," shrieked the queen. "Can't you fools see that?"

The king wondered if the queen was ill.

"Just look at her!" the queen cried.

The king gave the maid another look. And, come to think of it, she did look rather like the princess.

Rouget and Rojar were thinking the same thing.

Harold, on the other hand, who had already had this thought, was wondering if he might have to carry out another rescue. It seemed somewhat difficult under the circumstances.

"Do something!" the queen shrieked.

The king felt the heat of battle running through his veins. Here was his damsel in distress and there, the enemy. For just a moment, the excitement of the good old days came rushing back to him, and he was young and daring and he could do anything. With a great cry, he took a running start and leaped over the table.

"Save us!" cried the queen, clutching the tablecloth.

The king was not as agile as he thought he was. He landed on the tray of cookies with a crunch.

"The cookies!" wailed Rouget.

"How come he never does that with the vegetables?" his brother cried.

The king climbed off the table. He was cross. His pants were sticky and his teatime ruined.

"You!" he bellowed, pointing at Azula. "Don't you move!"

The old Azula just might have obeyed him. After all, she'd spent her whole life listening to kings.

But this was not the old Azula. This Azula figured she could choose which kings to listen to and which kings to ignore, and this, most certainly, was one to be ignored.

She took a small step forward. "Catch!" she cried, flinging the teapot in the air.

"My teapot!" gasped the queen.

"Guard!" yelled the king.

Then several things happened at once.

The king, much to his credit, caught the teapot.

Rouget snatched the last unbroken cookie.

Rojar grabbed a butter knife, which was the only weapon handy.

Harold slipped out a side door.

And a red knight rushed in. "I'm here to serve my king!" he cried.

"Arrest her," roared the red king. "Take her to the dungeon."

The knight seized Azula by the arm.

Now, you may notice this knight didn't say which king he served. And if you haven't yet guessed, I'll give you a hint: it wasn't the red king.

"Roderick!" gasped Azula as the red knight hustled her out of the room.

The brave knight Roderick nod-

ded. "At your service," he said. At long last, he had his princess rescue. "Ready to run?"

"Ready," said Azula.

And they ran.

The red castle wasn't only bigger than the blue castle, it was more complicated. Drawing rooms led into living rooms that led to libraries that led to corridors that led back to the drawing rooms. And so on.

"We are lost," said Roderick hopelessly, as he and Azula came across the picture gallery for the third time.

"Lost?"

The knight nodded, trying vainly to ignore the old red royalty that stared down from the paintings.

"We cannot be lost."

"And yet we are. I cannot find the way out."

"Then I will."

"I beg your pardon?"

"I will." And as Roderick watched, bewildered, the blue princess took Ralph's compass from her pocket and consulted it. "This way," she said, starting down the hallway. "To the southeast tower."

"We don't want a tower," Roderick patiently corrected her. "We want an exit."

The blue princess turned to look at him. "The southeast tower *is* an exit," she said.

"Is it?" Roderick sounded doubtful. "How on earth do you know this?"

"Because I've been there," said Azula, starting down the hall again. "Twice."

The brave knight Roderick hesitated. Surely he knew better than the princess how to find the way out. Or—perhaps he didn't. You see: he was learning, too. "Hold on!" he called, and hurried to catch up.

In no time, they reached the southeast tower. And, of course, they found the secret passage that led to the secret stairway that led to the secret exit.

"Outstanding," Roderick murmured as they headed for the door. He was impressed; the blue castle had nothing of the sort.

"What ho?" the guard said sleepily.

"Hail!" answered Azula.

And he waved them through. It was that simple.

And then, suddenly, it wasn't.

"Halt!" A red knight stepped in front of them. A real red knight.

CHAPTER TWELVE

The Beginning

Roderick drew his sword.

"Stand down," the red knight said, looking uncomfortable. "I mean you and the maid no harm." For he thought Roderick a red knight, and the blue princess but a kitchen maid.

"Then what can be the meaning of this?" Roderick threw his shoulders back and tried to sound important.

The red knight looked flustered.

"Well?" demanded Roderick. "Speak up."

At that moment, Rouget stepped out from behind the stairs.

"Oh brother," said Azula. "Not again."

The red prince drew himself up tall. "Just so you know," he said, "I'll never marry you."

"Do you mean that?" Azula asked him.

"I will marry a *real* princess," Rouget said. "You're too much trouble."

"Am I?" said Azula. And she smiled.

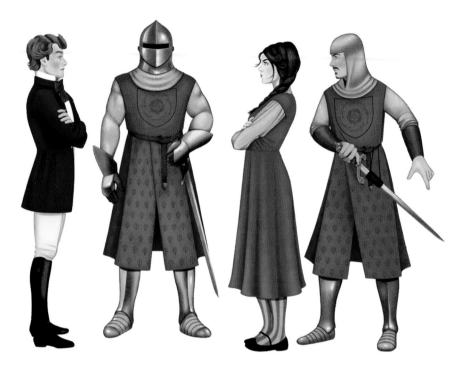

"Is that all?" asked Roderick.

Rouget glared at him. "That's all," he said. "Now go away."

"Your wish is our command," said Roderick sensibly.

The red knight stepped aside to let them pass. "My apologies," he murmured. "I don't know what got into him." He turned to Azula. "But it must be nice to be mistaken for a princess."

"I suppose it may have its advantages," Azula answered. "Though I cannot think of any of them at the moment."

"I say." Roderick turned to the red knight. "Might you be so kind as to deliver this?" He took a letter from his pocket. It had been addressed, with many fancy flourishes, to Bronwyn.

"I would be delighted to," the red knight said.

"Please give her my regards," Roderick continued, "and please tell her I'll return for her as soon as I am able."

"But of course you will return," the red knight said. "You serve your king."

"Indeed I do," said Roderick, offering Azula his arm.

And together, the two left the castle.

We must make haste," said Roderick, once the door had closed behind them. "The red prince may change his mind."

"Or the red king may wish to check on us."

The two looked out across the plains.

"It is a long way to our camp," Azula said.

"And many hours until nightfall." Roderick gazed around them at the land that stretched for mile after open mile. "There is no choice," he continued. "We will have to chance it."

As he spoke, there was a whinny. Roderick and Azula turned to find an old horse tied outside the door.

"Why, this is most convenient," Roderick said. "And yet—most strange." He frowned at something on the saddle.

"What is it?" Azula asked.

"It is—" he poked at it—"a mask."

Do you remember? When Azula tossed the teapot in the air, several things happened at once. The red queen cried out in alarm; the red king caught the teapot; Rouget ate a cookie; Rojar grabbed the butter knife; and Harold slipped out of the room. Now we know why.

"It is for us," Azula said, and blushed.

"Then let us ride it."

As the two rode off across the countryside, the masked man—who, without his mask, was simply Harold—watched them from the tower. Once or twice, he thought he saw Azula turn to look back, and he wondered if she had looked back for him. He hoped she had, just as he hoped that one day they might meet again.

But no prince has a crystal ball in which to see the future. In this instance, there is but a single person who can tell you what may happen and that person happens to be me. But that's a story for another day. In the meantime, let us finish this one.

The blue Princess Azula had a great deal to think about on the way home. As she and Roderick and their escorts journeyed back to the blue castle, she thought about the life a princess led. She thought of shopping expeditions, dinner parties, velvet frocks and sparkle polish; feather comforters and bubble baths and rich desserts with names like île flottante, and crème brûlée, and mousse au chocolat.

Then she thought about the wide blue sky, the hills and hollows of the countryside, the stars that glittered all night as she slept. She thought of peanut butter sandwiches and steam trains; secret stairs and toy swords; and, of course, she thought of the masked man; and as she thought, something inside her shifted and then settled.

She had seen a lot, our Princess Azula; more importantly, she'd learned a lot, not least about herself. The question, she finally realized, as she rode across the several kingdoms and one mountain range, was what she'd do with all that learning.

Azula was still thinking when the party rode into the castle. A great cheer went up, though mostly for the brave blue knight who'd spied on the red castle and then rescued the blue princess. He'd been bold and brave, while she had been—well, no one understood exactly what she'd been.

And life went on.

The king continued to be kingly, leading meetings, making rules, and meeting other rulers. Roderick was awarded a promotion which, with luck and proper funding, would allow him to sneak back to the red castle. And Azula, once again, returned to the life of a princess.

For the next few weeks, she went through the motions of her old existence, cutting ribbons, kissing babies, buying perfumes, planning parties. But her heart, which beat on strong and fast, just wasn't in it.

Then, one night, there was a full moon, and the moon reminded her of Ralph's round compass, which she now and then took out to study. The right time, she knew, had come at last. She closed the travel books she'd bought, and folded up her maps, and wrote a short note to her father who, she knew, would never understand.

Outside, the moon shone on the cobblestones and a barn owl hooted from its faraway perch. Quietly, Azula made her way to the main gate and tiptoed out. The compass, which she now wore on a necklace, gave her courage and no little comfort.

From the bridge over the moat, she turned around to look back at the castle that had been her home for all her life. Then, with the moon lighting her way, she hoisted her bag to her shoulder and went off to seek her fortune.

Glossary

ABSURD Ridiculous. A prince may think it is absurd to wait on someone, but what's actually absurd is that he thinks so.

AMBUSH A surprise attack.

ANTICIPATE Look forward to; expect.

ASSESSMENT An evaluation or measurement of something, as when you are given a reading assessment to see if you are able to read this book on your own.

BLACKMAIL A scheme to make a person do exactly as you wish.

BOEUF BOURGUIGNON Beef stew.

BRANDY A kind of wine, usually served after dinner in a glass called a snifter.

CAPPUCCINO A special kind of coffee with a lot of milk.

CHASTEN Or, more usually, to be chastened—To feel much as if you have been scolded and ought not to continue with whatever it is you've been doing.

CIVILIZED Elegant and orderly.

COLLEAGUES People with whom you work.

COMMITMENTS Obligations that must be satisfied, or activities that must be attended to.

COMMITTEE A bunch of knights sitting around, talking things over and making their plans.

CONSTERNATION Alarm or bewilderment, as when a princess does something her father thinks she oughtn't.

CONVENTIONAL Traditional; doing things as they have always been done, which is generally not a very interesting or exciting way of doing them. Often used to describe people who are unwilling to listen to new ideas.

COQUILLES SAINT-JACQUES Scallops in a cream sauce.

CRÈME BRÛLÉE Translated from the French as "burnt cream," crème brûlée is a custard dessert topped with caramelized sugar.

CRUCIAL Most important, as in the getting of a maiden's name.

DEFICIT More money going out than coming in. Never a good thing.

DELEGATION A bunch of knights sent elsewhere— often by a committee—to talk things over.

DISPATCH Send out.

DOODAD Stuff.

DUTY CALLS When chores must be done, baths taken, and other unpleasant tasks attended to.

ELATED Thrilled or overjoyed, which is what a princess is supposed to be—but isn't always—when a prince asks her to marry him.

ELIGIBLE Worthy, qualified, or suitable, as in being bold, courageous, daring, clever, trustworthy and resourceful, when that is just the sort of knight that's needed.

ESSENTIAL Absolutely necessary.

EXASPERATED Exceedingly annoyed.

EXPEDITION An outing or a trip, usually involving some kind of adventure.

FAMILIAR You know what you're getting.

FLOURISH Fancy handwritten decorations sometimes found on those out-of-date-but-lovely things called letters.

FORMAL Stiff or official, as opposed to warm and friendly.

FURTIVE Sneaky.

GOURMET Fit only for the finest palates, which is what a fancy person calls the way he tastes his food.

HEAVY-HANDED Making sure you get your way, which isn't usually the nicest strategy.

HERALDRY Flags and banners.

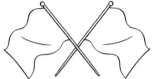

ÎLE FLOTTANTE A French confection translated as "floating island," this is a dessert made of meringue floating on vanilla custard. When done correctly, it resembles, as you might suppose, a floating island. Also known as oeufs à la neige, or eggs in snow, for a similar reason. Of course, you may believe it looks like something else entirely, in which case you are more than welcome to think up your own name for it.

IMPULSIVELY Without thinking too much, which is the best way to kiss someone.

INAPPROPRIATE Something that oughtn't be done, as when a princess takes on the job of a scout; or, more to the point, as when a knight believes she can't.

INCOME Money coming in. Always a good thing.

INSOLENCE A rude or disrespectful way of behaving, sometimes followed by the exclamation, "How dare you!"

INTERFERENCE Someone getting in your way. It's usually annoying.

INTERMEDIARY A go-between or middle person, which may be a very useful person for a kidnapper who wishes to remain unknown.

INTERNATIONAL RELATIONS How kings and kingdoms (and presidents and prime ministers) treat each other.

JUNCTURE Place or point, as in this juncture of the story.

KEEP ONE'S PRIDE INTACT Keep the same good opinion of yourself, as when a prince will go to any length to marry a princess, just to show he can.

LEVEL THE PLAYING FIELD Make both sides, or both teams, or both castles, equal.

MARKETING AND BRANDING How you tell the world exactly who you are.

MODEST Lacking in pizzazz; not flashy or show-offy.

MOUSSE AU CHOCOLAT Chocolate mousse—which happens to be one of my favorite desserts.

OBJECTION A reason for not doing something, as when a princess has an objection to marrying a prince who is pushy, bossy, selfish, and annoying, too.

OBLIGATION Something that must be done; a responsibility.

OPTIMISTIC Hopeful, as in I am optimistic you will understand this definition, which means that I think you will.

PARTY POOPER Someone who always sees the gloomy side of things; a pessimist.

PEEVISH Cross.

PERSONNEL Employees.

PINE Long for or miss very badly, which may happen when you don't see someone for a while. Also a kind of tree, though not in this story.

POLYGRAPH MACHINE A lie-detecting machine. Something many parents wish they owned, but fortunately don't.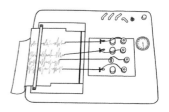

POMP AND CIRCUMSTANCE Splendid displays of heraldry.

PRECISE Accurate or exact, as when you are catching a train and need to get to the station at precisely one minute before the train departs.

PREDICAMENT A problematic situation, as when a prince attempts to marry a princess without her consent.

PROCLAMATION An important announcement, often used to describe almost anything a king tells his citizens.

PROMOTION A better job, usually with more money and a better title, as when a junior knight is upgraded to a senior knight.

PROPER FUNDING Having the necessary money, which is very helpful if you want to get things done.

PROPOSITION A plan or task that must be dealt with, like the running of a castle or the wearing of a dirty shirt. Note also: an unpleasant proposition is an idea that stinks.

QUALIFIED Having the knowledge or ability to do something.

QUICHE LORRAINE A tart with cheese and ham or bacon.

QUICKEN To make or become faster, as when your heartbeat quickens.

QUILL PEN A pen made from a feather. Not something you should generally make yourself.

REGRET A feeling of unhappiness or disappointment over something that's happened, or something that you wish had happened, but has not.

REMISS Careless; failing to pay attention to your task, as when a kitchen maid forgets to pour the tea.

REPUTATION What is said about you when you're not around.

REVELATION A sudden and surprising discovery.

SALARY The money you're paid for doing your job.

SCOFF To mock or make fun of in a not-very-nice way.

SELF-CONFIDENCE Belief in yourself.

SHELTERED LIFE You don't get out much, as when a princess never leaves her castle.

SOUS-CHEF The second-in-command cook.

STATIC Background noise that makes it hard to hear. Often an unwelcome feature of those old-fashioned devices known as radios.

TROWEL A small shovel.

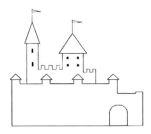

UNBEKNOWNST Not known, as when a prince neglects to tell his parents he will be marrying the princess they intend to exchange for ransom money.

WALLED CITY A city surrounded by walls.

WITHOUT A TRACE Unseen; leaving behind no evidence of a person's, or a thing's, presence. For example, when you finish with this book, you'll return it to the shelf and it will disappear without a trace. Or—better yet—it won't.